The Raven is a dark-colored, highly intelligent bird that is part of the crow family. Ravens reveal their presence by a deep, croaking call. They are strong, soaring fliers and are often seen doing aerial acrobatics along the rims and over the canyons, particularly during courtship. They love to tumble and somersault. Ravens typically build complex stick-nests on the cliff ledges and line the nests with moss, grass and bark. They are scavengers, and are often seen picking up almost anything.

I AM AN ARO PUBLISHING
60 WORD BOOK

MY 60 WORDS ARE:

a	ground	Roost
and	hang	saving
at	is	saw
back	it	shiny
bits	let's	string
blue	lots	Suzy
bottles	mirrors	swoosh
but	money	take
cans	no	the
Choosy	of	them
cloth	off	these
cones	old	things
door (doors)	on	tin
down	pick	to
flew	pine	too
floors	pins	up
for	put	use (used)
glass	Raven's	walls
grab (grabbed)	red	was
green	rocks	wood

GRAND CANYON CRITTERS

RAVEN'S ROOST

BY BOB REESE

 ARO PUBLISHING

Raven saw a shiny thing,
On the ground, on a string.

Raven flew down
and grabbed it, swoosh!
And flew it back
to Raven's Roost.

Raven's saving for no use,
Lots of things at Raven's Roost.

Pine cones, wood, rocks and tin,
Mirrors, money, glass and pins.

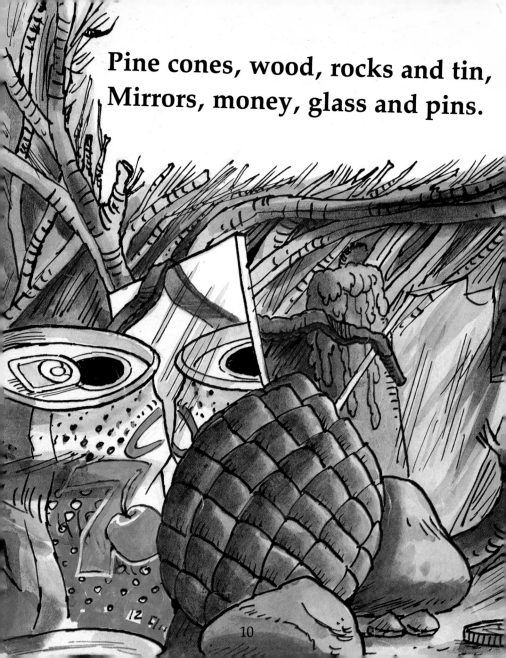

Bits of cloth, red, green and blue.

Old tin cans and bottles, too.

Raven's saving for no use,
Lots of things at Raven's Roost.

Suzy Choosy flew
to Raven's door.

Suzy Choosy saw
things on the floor.

"Let's take these things
and put them to use.

Let's use these things
at Raven's Roost."

"Let's pick them up off the floors,
Let's hang them on the walls and doors."

Raven was saving for no use,
But Suzy used things at Raven's Roost.

j 43 419